FLUFF THE FARTING FISH

*Also by Michael Rosen
and illustrated by Tony Ross:*

Burping Bertha

FLUFF THE FARTING FISH

MICHAEL ROSEN

illustrated by Tony Ross

Andersen Press
London

First published in 2013 by
Andersen Press Limited
20 Vauxhall Bridge Road
London SW1V 2SA
www.andersenpress.co.uk

2 4 6 8 10 9 7 5 3

Text copyright © Michael Rosen, 2013
Illustration copyright © Tony Ross, 2013

British Library Cataloguing in Publication Data available.

ISBN 978 1 84939 527 4

Printed and bound in Great Britain
by CPI Group (UK) Ltd, Croydon, CR0 4YY

Elvie wanted a puppy. She said to her mum, "I want a puppy."

Mum said, "Yes."

What?!!!

Really????

A puppy???

And she said yes????!!!

How brilliant is that???!!!!

The next day Mum went out to get the puppy.

What?!!!

Really????

A puppy???

Yes!!!

How brilliant is that????!!!!

And she came back with the puppy.

What?!!! Really???? A puppy???

Well, actually, er . . . no.

She came back with . . .

...A fish.

A fish????

"But, Mum," said Elvie, "I don't want a fish. I want a puppy."

"Never mind," said Mum. "You'll soon get used to it."

So Elvie put the fish in her room.

She called it Fluff, just in case it started getting fluffy and turned into a puppy.

And then she started to get Fluff to do puppy things.

She dropped little sticks into Fluff's tank and shouted,

Sometimes Fluff would go and get the stick. Especially if the stick was made of fish food.

Elvie waved her fingers around in
the air above the water and shouted,

And sometimes Fluff would leap up and try to grab her fingers. Especially if there were bits of fish food on her fingers.

She frowned, wagged her finger and shouted,

Fluff didn't ever sit. Fluff wasn't good at sitting at all.

Then Elvie had a brilliant idea. She saw someone on the TV who had a dog that barked at numbers – and it barked the right number of times!

So Elvie held up numbers at the side of Fluff's tank, and shouted.

She didn't mind ever so much if Fluff didn't actually go, "Woof!" but she did rather hope that maybe Fluff would blow a bubble.

But, no. Nothing.
But Elvie didn't give up.
Oh, no.

Every day she stood by the tank and shouted.

But not even a bubble . . .

Until . . .
Until . . .

One day . . .

Something amazing happened.

Instead of a bubble coming out of Fluff's mouth — a bubble came out of Fluff's <u>bum</u>.

Yes.

Fluff *farted*, and a little bubble floated up to the surface of the water.

What?!!! Really???? Oh yes!

Elvie tried again.

And, yes, what do you know?! Fluff
blew another bubble.

Elvie shouted,

"Bark!"
"Bark!"

And, yes, Fluff farted twice.

Elvie jumped up and down in excitement.

And she rewarded Fluff with her favourite fish food.

Then Elvie tried something else, she held up the number 3.

"Look, Fluff!"

she shouted. **"Three!"**

And, yes, the incredible thing happened: Fluff farted three times.

Three little bubbles floated up to the surface.

What?!!!
Really????
Oh yes!

So now every day was another exciting day with Fluff.

Every day Elvie taught Fluff another trick with bubbles.

Fluff was farting twice, three times, four times.

Do you know something?
Fluff even started to do sums.

"Two plus two!" shouted

Elvie.

And sure enough, Fluff answered
with four bubbles!
Incredible.
Amazing.
Wonderful.

Then Elvie had another thought.

What if Fluff could make the bubbles sound different – low ones and high ones – just like when she sang in school?

So Elvie started singing training.

Elvie would sing a note and say, "Fluff, go!"

And it wasn't long before Elvie could hear that Fluff's bubbles were the notes that Elvie sang.

She sang low . . . and Fluff made
a bubble-sound low.

She sang high . . . and Fluff made
a bubble-sound high.

You know what that meant, don't you?

It wasn't long before Fluff could fart
whole tunes, whole songs.

The first song Elvie taught her was
"Baa baa Black Sheep".

Then she taught Fluff "Yellow Submarine".

Then she taught Fluff, "The Sun Has Got His Hat On".

What?!!! Really???? Oh yes!

One day, Elvie was watching TV and she saw that they were looking for people to come along for a talent show.

I know, thought Elvie. *I could take Fluff along, and get her to sing.*

So, that's what she did.

Elvie took Fluff to the TV studios.

"I've got a fish that can sing," she told them.

"Yes, yes, dear, of course you have," they said, not believing her.

"I have," she said.

As she was so young, the judges said that they would let her go on to the stage and show the people her fish but that was all. Just showing. No singing.

"Yes, yes, dears," said Elvie to them. "Of course."

She waited and waited while the other acts went on:

Jeff the Juggler who could take out his eyes and juggle them.

Wally the Worm Wiggler who made it look as if he could feed worms in through one ear and pull them out the other.

TV Man who climbed into his TV and sang the National Anthem looking out from inside his TV set.

Then it was Elvie's turn.

She walked on to the stage with Fluff.

She bowed.

And then she turned to the fish tank and shouted:

Everyone laughed. How ridiculous. How silly. How could a fish sing?!!!

But then, even as they laughed, they could see the bubbles rising up out of Fluff's bum.

Amazing, incredible Fluff was farting "The Sun Has Got His Hat On".
The audience held their breath in amazement.

And then at the end, they stood up and burst into applause, whooping and whistling for Elvie and her farting fish.

They loved them both.

Well, you know what's coming, don't you . . .?

Fluff went on to win the talent show.

Fluff became the most famous fish in the world.

Everyone wanted to see and hear Fluff the Farting Fish.

Soon Fluff was being asked to appear at music festivals, playing with top stars.

She was asked to sing in operas.

She was asked to sing at huge concerts with whole orchestras.

Then one day something so awful, so bad and so sad happened.

Elvie and Fluff were doing a show with . . . yes . . . a puppy.

And you'll remember that Elvie wanted a puppy.

Now, you're not going to believe this, but this puppy was called, yes, Fluff.

This is what happened:

Elvie came to the front of the stage and, just as she always did, to get Fluff ready she shouted,

'Fluff!'

Fluff the fish perked up, got herself ready to blow some bubbles . . .

Then Fluff the dog leaped up too.

He had escaped from his owner's hands and came bounding up to Elvie and Fluff the fish.

Before Elvie could notice Fluff the dog, she called out to Fluff the fish, "Sing 'Take me, I'm yours'!"

Fluff started to blow her bubbles to the tune of "Take me, I'm yours".

And do you know what happened next?

Fluff the dog heard, "Take me, I'm yours", and so he did.

He jumped into the tank, opened his mouth and . . .

in went Fluff the fish.

The world's most famous, the world's richest, the world's most successful fish was in a dog's mouth.

What? Really? No! Oh yes!

What could be done?

Any second now Fluff was going to be swallowed, and the whole amazing story of Fluff the Farting Fish would end. There would be no more singing, no more bubbles, no more Fluff.

Elvie was horrified. She stood rooted to the spot like a frozen tree.

Then a thought flew into her mind.

If she just did some kind of puppy-training thing, just as she had done all that time ago when she first got Fluff, her amazing farting fish would be saved.

She held out her hand above Fluff the dog's head.

She shouted:

And . . .

Fluff the dog jumped . . .

And as Fluff the dog jumped.

Fluff the dog opened his mouth.

And as Fluff the dog opened his mouth . . .

Fluff the fish jumped out.
And went flying through the air in
a beautiful rainbow shape.

Landing back in the tank with a big...

SPLOSH

Shouted Elvie, and Fluff the dog sat
down.

While Fluff the fish tried yet again
to sit down . . .

But, as we know, that was one trick
she couldn't do.

Never mind that, though.
Fluff the fish had been saved.
Amazing.
Wonderful.
Incredible.
Hooray!
But . . .
But . . .
But . . .

When – and it is not going to make
you happy to hear this . . .

When – and it is not going to make
you jump for joy to hear this . . .

When Elvie turned to Fluff and shouted:

There was nothing.

Not a thing.

Not a sound.

Not a bubble.

Not even the smallest, tiniest, weeniest leak of air that could make even the smallest, tiniest, weeniest sound.

There was nothing.

Nothing at all.

★

From that day then till this day now Fluff has never sung another song, has never blown another bubble, has never farted another fart.

Fluff is silent, still and quite, quite quiet.

But, of course, Elvie still loves Fluff.

And Fluff still loves Elvie.

They are happy, happy, happy, the girl and Fluff her fish.

And, I've heard – this may not be absolutely true, it may be a fib – but I did hear it . . . so I might as well tell you.

I heard that Elvie was learning how to do what Fluff did.

You know . . . sing out of her . . . you-know-what . . .

Do you think she will?

Do you think she will be able to learn how to do it?

I wonder . . .

Jamela's Dress

Story & Pictures by
Niki Daly

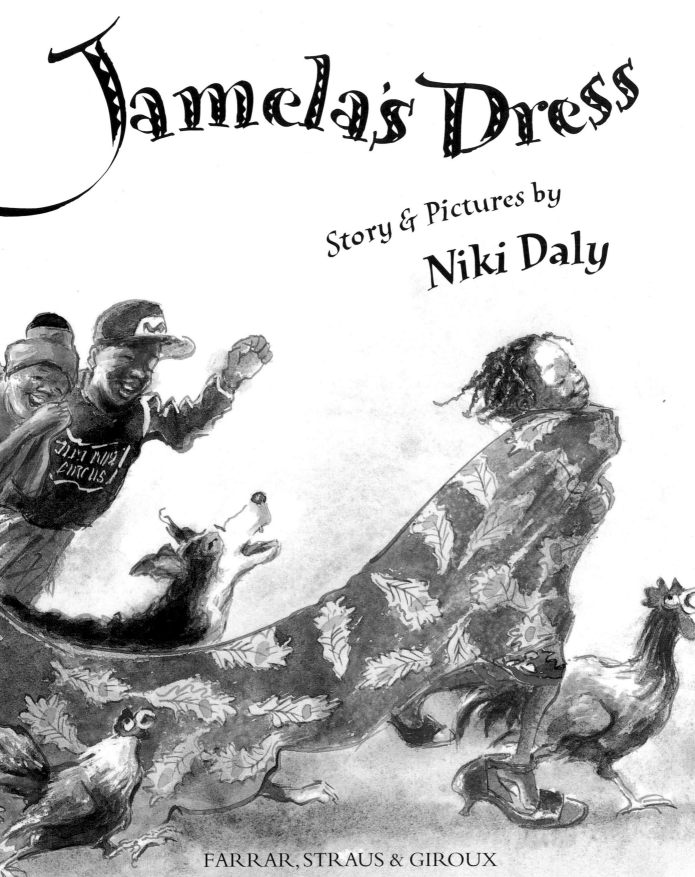

FARRAR, STRAUS & GIROUX
New York

Mama was very pleased with the new material she'd found at Mnandi's. She had worked hard to earn the money for it.

"It's beautiful, Mama," said Jamela, stroking the crisp new material.

"Yes, it's beautiful. It costs a lot of money—but I need something special to wear for Thelma's wedding," said Mama.

Jamela helped Mama wash the stiffness out of the new material. Together they hung it up to dry.

"I'll look after it, Mama," said Jamela.

"Thank you," said Mama. "Just make sure Taxi doesn't jump up and dirty my material."

"Okay," said Jamela.

A warm breeze blew. Jamela rubbed her cheek against the soft material and followed the beautiful patterns with her finger.

When Taxi barked, Mama called, "Jamela, are you looking after my material?"

"Yes, Mama. It's getting nice and dry," said Jamela.

Dreamily, Jamela swayed between the folds of material as they flapped and wrapped around her into a dress.

When Mama heard nothing going on, she called,
"Are you looking after my material, Jamela?"
There was no answer.

Down the road went Jamela, proud as a peacock,
to show Thelma her beautiful dress for the wedding.

She passed Miss Style hairdressers and the Snak-Pak grocery.
"Hi, beautiful!" called old Greasy Hands, who was fixing up
Thelma's wedding car.

Children sang,

Kwela Jamela African Queen!

Taxi barked, and Mrs. Zibi's chicken went wild.

Then a boy on a bicycle, who wasn't looking where he was going, went skidding all over Mama's dress material.

What a show!

In his photo studio, Archie heard the commotion.
He ran out, clutching his special camera, and shouted,
"Hold it, Jamela!"

So Jamela posed. The children pushed in. Taxi pushed in. Mrs. Zibi and her chicken pushed in. And the boy on the bicycle just s-q-u-e-e-z-e-d in. They all smiled.

But when Thelma saw Jamela, she scolded, "Haai, Jamela!
Your mama's going to be *verrrry* upset when she sees
what you've done with her material."

And Mama was. Mama was so upset that she couldn't even look
at Jamela. She just looked at the dirty, torn material and said sadly,
"What am I going to wear for the wedding?"

Everyone felt sorry for Mama and cross with Jamela. Even Jamela
was cross with Jamela. She hadn't meant to ruin Mama's material.
It just happened.

A few days later, Archie saw Jamela coming down the road without her usual smile. He called, "Hey, Jamela, why so sad? Come see the good news." Pointing to a front-page photograph in the newspaper, Archie read proudly:

"KWELA JAMELA
AFRICAN QUEEN—
*a prize-winning photograph
taken by Archie Khumalo.*"

But instead of looking happy, Jamela started to cry—and she told Archie all about Mama's messed-up material.

"That's a sad, sad story, Jamela," said Archie, "but it has a happy ending." He put his hand into his bag. Jamela wiped her eyes.

"See," said Archie, taking out a bundle of money. "I won big bucks for that photograph."

Jamela had never seen so much money.

"You can buy lots of things at the shops with that money, Archie," said Jamela.

"Right!" Archie laughed. "That's the happy ending."

In the afternoon, Archie arrived carrying a gift for Jamela's mama.

"What is this, Archie?" Mama asked in surprise.

"Open it, Mama, open it!" cried Jamela.

Mama unwrapped the parcel. Inside was a beautiful piece of material from Mnandi's—just like the first piece.

Jamela jumped up and down.

"*Enkosi kakhulu.* Thank you, Archie!" said Mama.

"No, you must thank Kwela Jamela African Queen,"
said Archie, holding up his prize-winning photograph.

When Mama saw it, she gave Jamela a big hug.

After Archie had gone, Jamela helped Mama
wash the material and hang it up to dry.
"It's the most beautiful material in
the world," said Jamela.
Mama just smiled.
They sang songs as they
watched the feathery patterns
dance in the warm breeze.

Then Mama and Jamela played
a hand-clapping game
for a while.

"Let's do teapots, Mama!" cried Jamela.
So Jamela taught Mama to do
a little song
about a teapot
with a spout.
They dipped
and tipped
and the tea
poured out.

When they stopped, the material felt warm and
dry. So Mama showed Jamela how to fold it—just as
she had learned to do it when she was a little girl.

That evening, Mama cut and sewed until she had her special dress to wear to Thelma's wedding. When she finished, there was a piece of material left over.

Mama measured it with her eye, this way and that way. Then she looked at sleeping Jamela and smiled.

The hands of the clock passed midnight, and Mama was still hard at work. Every now and then she sang softly to herself, "Kwela Jamela African Queen."

Next day at the wedding, Thelma looked radiant.